Croc-Shifter

By David G Evans

Table of Contents

A long time ago there was a tribe called the San tribe, who saved the nuerbers tribe from many unforeseen dangers. The leader of the nuerbers tribe, allowed his people to practice spells and magic.

The nuerbers tribes people, enjoyed dancing among other activities. They would construct these weapons Rungu, Zulu shields, Zulu spears, and Maasai spears.

Their diet would consist of a mixture of vegetables, legumes, and sometimes meat. One of the people in the tribe, made bread from the extra grains that they had.

After consuming the bread, the hunters of the tribe went out hunting. When they came back later, one of the children had fallen ill.

Then the witch doctor was summoned from his dwelling, he quickly went over to where the child was. The child was laying on his side complaining of pain in his back, and his feet.

The father of the boy kept telling him, you better save my boy. At once the witch doctor began making up a potion, out of the ingredients that he brought with him.

Suddenly the boy went into a dream, he dreamt that he was swimming in the river. He was talking to his mother, suddenly a hunter came after him with a spear.

Chapter 1

He dodged the spear and ran out of the water, only to find himself being chased by a giant crocodile.

The crocodile swung his powerful tail and hit the hunter killing him, then there was a pack of hyenas chasing around tribes men in front of him.

He yelled out everything leave me alone, then he dreamt that he had fallen into quicksand. That's when he opened his eyes and saw that everything was okay.

The witch doctor handed him something to eat, you must eat this to get better. Then the boy's father chimed in, you should feel better soon after this. I know that it doesn't taste the best, but it's going to make you better.

Tell us everything that you are feeling, I'm seeing things. That's probably just a side effect of the potion, I saw a hyena standing in front of me. I want to run around with the other children, you can but today you have to rest.

I wish that my mother was here with me right now, she's cooking for our feast later. Tonight, we'll celebrate a successful hunt.

I wish I could go with the hunters one day, you will but you're too young yet. I don't like to talk about your brother but I need to talk about him to make an example for you.

"Do you remember the day that he went missing?"

"Yes," and a tear began to run down his cheek.

You and him used to play so nicely together, he would have made such a strong warrior. I can still remember, when one of our hunters was run down by a lion.

That was a rogue lion, and I'm the one who killed him. This scar on my arm was from fighting with the lion, and it's something I'll never forget.

Suddenly they could hear the tribesmen yelling, I'll be back soon I have to go check on my people. A hippo came running towards one of the huts, another tribesman said get out of there. The people fled from their hut; the hippos head got stuck inside the hut.

It went over to a tree and slammed into it hoping that it could break loose, and it did. Then it saw a young woman and chased after her, not so far away there was a leopard in a tree feasting on its prey.

The woman soon came to a tree and immediately climbed up it. She could no longer see her village and was very worried. The hippo soon gave up trying to get her it went back into the water, close by was a herd of gazelle.

Then she heard a growl in the distance, that's when the hairs on the back of her neck stood up. After quite some time she climbed down out of the tree but was still very vigilant.

She hollered out, I'm very much in need right now. Moments later a leopard, had climbed down out of the tree. He was stalking one of the children in the tribe, the boy quickly ran into one of the huts where his mother was.

I always tell you not to venture out too far, you're young and vulnerable to predators. You need to stay in here awhile until the predators go away, but my father is out there. He knows how to defend himself against predators and is very skilled with using his weapons.

> "When he gets too old to hunt will he pass the spear down to me?"

> "I'm sure that he will."

When I'm old enough to become a hunter, I want to hunt down a leopard. You realize that you could die from hunting dangerous game, I know all about the dangers.

In the hut next door, a mother was nursing her baby. A snake came crawling out of the grass, it was slithering a long towards the young mother.

Eventually the snake came crawling into the hut, the mother kept a hold of her baby and grabbed her spear. The snake went to strike her, she hit it the head with the spear.

It seemed to be just stunned so she dropped the spear and grabbed her knife and slit off its head. Two young women were down by the river, their boyfriends were happily splashing around in the river. Little did they know that they would be having a life-or-death struggle. Two snakes crawled down the bank of the river and entered the water.

They quickly swam over to the men, both snakes went after one man. He frantically went running out of the water, he tried to get their fangs out of his flesh but failed.

His friend got out of the water and grabbed a stick, and started whacking the snakes in their heads, that only left them confused.

He saw something that was sticking out of a bush nearby, he quickly went over there and saw that it was a spear and picked it up.

While his friend tried eagerly to get the snakes off him but nothing worked. The women were so terrified that they didn't make a move. He ran over to his buddy and began cutting the snakes necks with the sharp part of the spear.

Luckily he was able to cut their heads off and pull them off of his arm. They were both out of breath, and when they went to look for the women they were both gone.

Even though the snakes were dead his health was still in danger, the fangs of the snakes left deep lacerations in the muscle in his arm.

As they were walking back to the village, they heard the vocalizations of a mother and baby crocodile.

We must find and kill both of those crocodiles; the mother is an immediate threat to our village. I don't think the baby should be killed, but after we kill it's mother it's going to die anyway.

"Where are you going?"

"To look at these crocodile tracks by the river."

You're worrying about tracks while my arm is throbbing, we need to get to the witch doctor . Were just gatherers, not hunters. Let the hunters hunt it down, the more you mess around the better chance of us getting attacked by something else.

I've seen elephants come down to this river to take a drink, I don't feel like getting charged by an elephant.

 My wound has left me in a weakened state, I'm in no shape to run away from a predator. The wounded man got down onto the ground and put his head into the ground.

I don't feel any vibrations on the ground, so we are safe. Both of them saw an enemy tribesmen off in the distance and hid in the tall grass. I have lost some blood and I'm afraid I'm going to faint.

If that man would have saw us he would have beaten us both up and left us for dead. There were hyenas nearby that picked up on the smell of blood, I just heard the calls of a hyena.

We need to get out of here right now regardless of that enemy tribesman. The wounded man and his friend, they staggered back to the village.

A few hyenas were tracking closely behind them and arrived at the village. A tribeswoman was gathering up herbs, when she saw the hyenas.

The only thing that she had to attack them with was her spear, she dropped the herbs and ran after the hyenas. As she was going after the hyenas, the hunters came running out of there huts and joined in the fight.

Chapter 2

She stabbed one of the hyenas twice, then broke the spear over its head. One of the many hunters was armed with a makeshift bow and arrow.

He fired an arrow that stuck an already injured hyena. The hyena soon collapsed, while the other remaining hyenas ran off into the savannah.

There were a herd of elephants walking along the savannah, when the mother elephant saw the hyenas, she immediately guarded her baby. The hyenas were licking at their wounds, and groaning.

A young bull elephant and a mature bull began going at it, the young bull charged but missed the other elephant and slammed into one of the dying hyenas. In an instant the hyena's body was crushed, and it laid there lifeless.

The young bull used its trunk to investigate the body, and soon lost interest and the mature elephant overly exerted itself and had a heart attack. It collapsed, the young elephant went over to the fallen elephant and touched it with his trunk.

Then the rest of the herd came over to see what had happened, they realized that the elephant was dead, and they all mourned.

One of the hunters had saw this and told the entire tribe to come out and see what was going on. Sometime later the entire tribe was observing the elephants, they too felt bad for the death of the elephant.

After a while the herd of elephants went on, looking for another place to graze. The hunters began quartering up the elephant, when two enemy tribesmen spotted them. They backed away from the elephant and got their weapons ready.

Both tribes fiercely clashed, the hunter fiercely stabbed one of the enemy tribesman with his spear and knocked him to the ground. The other tribesman got punched in the face and stabbed in the neck and fell over dead.

The hunters raised their arms in victory. Then went back to carving up the elephants carcass, several buzzards came flying over to them.

The hunters chased away the buzzards so that they could focus on cutting up the elephant in peace. All the hunters and the gatherers went back to the village before nightfall, Madalitso had already gathered the wood earlier that day, for the giant fire that they were going to have. Rudo brought in a small crocodile, that they were going to worship that night.

While Rutendo was chopping up chicken to give to the crocodile, this was to appease the crocodile God Runta Montis.

The crocodile's mouth was tied shut with rope, until there ready to start the ceremony. The crocodile hissed and swung it's tail at Rudo, but he dodged his tail.

Rutendo brought a large bowl full of pieces of raw chicken and set it beside Rudo. Lerato went around the village gathering up the children, who were playing happily among each other.

Come on children we're having a ceremony tonight let's get gathered in the sacred area. Eventually all the children were gathered up and were now sitting in a circle in the sacred area.

Makena went around to check on the elderly people of the village, the one elderly man was sitting in his tent staring at the ants that were crawling around his food bowl.

When she sat down next to him, he suddenly stared over at her and said a creature of mystical powers will be awakened.

She ran out of the man's hut and went over to an elderly woman's hut who was making bread. Hello Tinonaa, she smiled at her. Every time I come to visit you, your always baking something.

"Would you mind if I sat next to you?"

"No," I wouldn't.

My grandchildren are so precious, I enjoy teaching them new things. My morning didn't go so well, I had to chase away a badger. I find myself having to take more naps then usual, you'll be just fine.

"Has your neighbor been acting strange?"

"No," not that I know of.

When I went in to check on him, he was staring. Don't pay no heed to what he says, I know it's scary what he says sometimes.

Just the other day he said that I was going to have a nightmare about giant snakes and I never had a nightmare.

His 5 kids sometimes come to visit me, and I give them bread. One of his children was in the river, when there was a hyena nearby.

His brother chased away the hyena and took the boy to a safer place. I hope that you have a good night of sleep, I will thanks.

"Have you ever gone to see the ceremony?"

"Yes."

Ever since I was 6 years old I have gone to see it. I'll help you to get there, I'd rather keep to myself.

I better be on my way to the ceremony, just be careful. Makena walked down a muddy path, and soon came to the ceremony area.

Everyone seemed to be so hyped for the ceremony, Makena quietly sat down. Now everyone in the village except for the elderly people gathered there. Someone yelled out why aren't we starting already? A woman answered him, we're waiting on Sipho.

A man yelled out; can't he ever be on time. Maybe he's just getting senile, then they saw a spirit go past them and everyone quieted down.

Rudo was just minding his own business and two small crocodiles came peacefully walking over to him. The massive flame of the fire, suddenly the flames almost went out. Sipho and the witch doctor arrived together.

Sipho sat down on his throne, and the witch doctor sat down next to him. Rudo brought the crocodile and the 2 others followed him, they stayed calmer then he thought they would.

Sipho stood up and said now we begin the ceremony, then the witch doctor stood up. They were ready to start there ceremonial dance, when a bloodied man came running over to Sipho. In a frantic voice, he pointed to the large crocodile.

That crocodile is cursed, and if you do your ceremony, the crocodile will turn into a mysterious creature called a shapeshifter.

It'll have the power to conquer and destroy anything. Allow your witch doctor to tell you about it, I got attacked by a hyena on my way here to warn you, if you proceed you will be attacked by the shapeshifter and killed. A boy from the audience got up and walked over to them, there's nothing to see here boy, go ahead back to where you were. Sipho was becoming more irritated by the minute.

The injured man went over to the crocodiles and tried to drag the big crocodile away. Suddenly a man from the audience came angrily charging after the injured man, knocking him to the ground. You're lying, your just a fear monger.

How dare you come here; you don't belong here. Sipho said to the man who was yelling at the injured, stop this madness.

Chapter 3

Your way out of line, you shouldn't be acting this way in front of the children. Your being a child yourself, stop trying to start trouble.

The man became even more enraged, and took a swing at Sipho, who ducked and his fist hit the witch doctor in the forehead causing him to fall down.

One of the small crocodiles snapped it's jaws at the injured man, the man ran off to the witch doctor's hut. The enraged man went back to where he came from, still fuming.

Some of the parents took away the children from the ceremony, some of the tribesmen said to one another that Sipho should be forced out as being an inept leader.

The tribesmen began to pelt Sipho with rocks and sticks. Then all the tribesmen yelled out if you don't do the ceremony were going to carve you up and feed you to the crocodiles. Out of nowhere a spear went flying past his head, get started someone shouted.

The children that we're left there, just closed their eyes and tried to remain calm. The witch doctor ran out of there as quickly as he could and didn't look back.

Sipho began doing the dance around the crocodiles, the small crocodiles were hissing and snapping their jaws, while the large, cursed crocodile remained calm.

Two tribesmen were talking, my grandfather used to say that the one neighboring tribes would curse crocodiles.

I never really believed it or even thought about it, to me it's just a legend. I told you what I think, now tell me what you think. I'm on the same page you are, I don't believe it.

It's ashame that we have to scare our leader into doing the ceremony, I think that he's just lost his mind. It appears that he's having trouble balancing while dancing, he's just a wreck.

I doubt he'll be still standing by the end of the dance. Maybe you should take over dancing for him, no I'm not going to help him.

"How many more times does he have to dance around the crocodiles?"

"Eight more times"

When this ceremony is over I'm going to chase that injured man out of here.

"Are you going to come with me while I chase him away?"

"No."

I'm going to spend time with my coming-of-age son. Tomorrow I'm going to show him how to bait in a predator, just leave that injured man alone he'll die from his wounds, you shouldn't talk like that. I don't ever want to hear that again, but it's true.

Sipho had completed the dance, both the small crocodiles ran off. Before his very eyes the cursed crocodile, shapeshifted into a fierce warrior with golden painted stripes going down his forehead and cheeks.

There was a dot of gold paint on the tip of his nose with a golden choker around his neck. He was armed with a long knife with a cobra head as the handle.

When the people sitting in the audience saw this, they ran away. One of the parents couldn't find their child who had run off into the darkness, they could hear the vocalization of a leopard. They searched all around and found their child hiding in the high grass.

The shapeshifter began to attack whomever it saw, someone began throwing rocks at him. Sipho narrowly escaped the shapeshifter, he ran as quickly as his legs would carry him. He seeked refuge in a mud hut, for the night.

The shapeshifter quickly caught up to the man grabbing him by his throat and stabbing him to death.

A woman saw him and screamed, she quickly retreated back into her hut closing the makeshift door behind her.

The shapeshifter shoved his knife through the door, the woman held her hand in front of her mouth trying not to scream.

One of the hunter men was nearby and saw what was happening, he charged at the shapeshifter with a spear.

But the spear just went right through him, the shapeshifter grabbed him by the head and cut his throat.

The woman took this time and escaped out the back of her hut. She just kept running, and even passed the village.

Now everyone left the village and fled to a safer area. The shapeshifter continued on killing animals and people, there were three hunters hiding out near the village watching the shapeshifter.

We must stop that thing at all costs, but you saw what it did to that hunter over there. Yes but there's three of us, we should be able to overpower him.

You're not getting my point; the hunters spear went right through him. We need to discuss this with the witch doctor.

I was looking forward to attacking him, don't worry we're going to find a way to stop him. Perhaps we should shoot a flaming arrow at him, that would just provoke him and he would come after us.

I don't know about you, but I don't have a death wish. Meanwhile the injured man, collapsed and his body began to shake violently.

His bruised body transformed into a 2 headed white lion, he left out a roar and tore out of the hut.

The hunters heard the roar and stood there quietly. I don't want to see what made that roar; we need to move now.

He wasn't watching where he was going, and his head bumped into a bees nest. Bees came pouring out of the nest, one of the hunters made a sound, and the shapeshifter heard it.

He immediately looked over there way but looked the other way when he heard something in the opposite direction. I thought for sure he was going to come over here and come after us, we're definitely lucky.

That sound that you heard was the call of a male lion, and it sounded close by. Hopefully the lion is smart enough to avoid the shapeshifter.

"Did anyone of you see Rutendo?"

"Yes," I witnessed her fleeing the village.

She probably joined back with her family by now.

"Where are we going to hide out overnight?"

"In the shelter by ocantiso's garden."

I thought Sipho banned everyone from going there, he's not here right now so he can't ban us.

"Remember how he said this place was so evil?"

"Yes."

He said that it was evil because crops won't grow here, one time one of the children went missing around here.

"Were they ever able to find the child?"

"No," they weren't.

Chapter 4

My opinion is that a lion or hyena got the child, I'm sure you're right. The hunters froze when they saw a double headed white lion, walk past them, they made sure that it was good and gone before they ran into the shelter to hide.

There's a lot more predators around here than they thought there was, I've never seen a lion like that in my life.

It must be deformed or something, but it was twice the size of a regular lion. I'm just glad that it didn't have one of our tribesmen in its mouth.

"Where do you think it's headed?"

"He's probably headed to another village, looking for food."

Hopefully the shapeshifter doesn't come anywhere near here tonight, seeing it during the days is scary enough but I can't imagine seeing it at night.

"Do you know if that thing will come after us in our dreams?"

"I don't think so."

I know that I'll be okay because I don't dream, just stop thinking about it and you'll no longer be afraid. The hunters settled in and fell asleep for the night.

While they were resting the shapeshifter, was focused on tracking the lion. He walked on for half a mile and was expecting to find a lion there, but there was no sign of it.

A snake came slithering up to the shapeshifter, when he saw it he cut off its head and left it lay. A buzzard landed on a carcass; the shapeshifter threw his knife at it. The knife chopped off the buzzards head, the shapeshifter walked further along.

Soon there were no more tracks to follow, he looked in the river thinking the cat was hiding in there.

The two headed lion was observing him from a far, it was hiding behind a hut. The shapeshifter left the river and went towards the hut that the lion was behind.

The lion waited there until the shapeshifter was close enough to strike, the 2 headed lion took his chances and fiercely attacked the shapeshifter.

The lion knocked the knife out of the shapeshifters hand, the shapeshifter punched the lion in his face.

The Lion just shook it off and swung its massive paw hitting the shapeshifter causing him to lose his balance.

The shapeshifter rolled down an embankment, the minute he got up the lion jumped up into the air and slammed down on top of him. The shapeshifter tried grabbing the lion by his throat, the lion let out a roar.

The shapeshifter made a serious effort to find it's knife but couldn't. The shapeshifter had become very angered and tried to punch the lion in its side but the lion grabbed his arm trying to break it but the shapeshifter arm was too strong.

He kicked dirt up into the lion's eyes, then the lion slammed him into a tree. Some branches fell down on top of him, but he easily brushed them off himself.

The lion started walking away from him, the shapeshifter followed him to a deep part in the river.

There were ten crocodiles around the river, two of them were larger than the rest. The shapeshifter tried to stab the lion with a stick, the lion slammed into him knocking, him into the river. Suddenly dozens of snakes, from the land came into the water.

The snakes began wrapping themselves around his arms and legs, he was able to stab one of them with a stick causing it to fall off of him.

The largest snake in the group bit into the back of his neck, he grabbed two more snakes and broke them in half.

There were still two snakes on him, the lion slammed into his back knocking him face down into the water.

All the snakes were now on him, he spoke some kind of spell and all the snakes were all thrown off of him.

The crocodiles began snapping their jaws at him, suddenly the water turned into a big wave and slammed into the crocodiles.

The crocodiles recovered and soon we're back after him, the shapeshifter crushed 2 of the snakes head. The rest of snakes that were still alive retreated back where they came from.

One of the crocodiles took the shapeshifter's hand into its mouth and tried to rip it off, but nothing happened.

The shapeshifter then tore off the crocodiles bottom jaw and threw it at the other crocodiles. Two of the larger crocodiles hit him with their tails, he grabbed one of the large crocodiles by its tail and swung it.

The crocodile still had plenty of fight in them, shapeshifter grabbed a hold of a yearling crocodile and threw it at the lion.

The lion tried to hold the shapeshifters head down in the water, but he overpowered the lion and slammed a river rock into the side of the lion. The lion groaned in agony from the pain inflicted on it.

Then the shapeshifter took the same rock and slammed it down onto one of the crocodiles head knocking it out.

A villager with a bow and arrow saw what was happening and fired two arrows at once at the shapeshifter.

Amazingly enough the shapeshifter caught one of the arrows and threw it back towards the villager who then ran off.

A pack of wild dogs came to the water's edge, all the commotion didn't seem to bother them. A crocodile came up and grabbed one of the wild dogs front foot and dragged it into the water.

The shapeshifter took a stick that he found and shoved it through the roof of the mouth of that crocodile.

Then he grabbed the crocodiles leg and broke it, then another crocodile grabbed ahold of that crocodiles tail and began to chew on it. The shapeshifter grabbed both crocodiles by their tails and threw them out of his way.

Next the shapeshifter went after the lion again, then another male line showed up. This lion charged after him, he tried to put his sharp teeth into his shoulder but his skin was as strong as steel. The shapeshifter punched the lion in its jaw, but this still didn't deter it.

The lion came back for more, the shapeshifter grabbed the lion by its throat and punched it in the eye.

One of the crocodiles opened its mouth and bit the lion in its leg, causing it to let out a roar. Then the lion retreated and laid down and licked its wounds. While this was going on the witch doctor was making a potion that he put some spell elixir into.

He made a potion that would stun the shapeshifter and freeze his body. Then the final potion, would send him back to the underworld where he belongs.

Chapter 5

The shapeshifter ran out of time as the warrior and transformed back into a 45-foot crocodile, in this form he could get injured.

The two headed lion, tried to get to the belly of the crocodile. The giant crocodile grabbed a hold of another crocodile and bit it in half.

Sipho had awakened after having a dream that he was falling off a cliff and before he opened his eyes he saw the shapeshifter. Once his eyes were open, he looked around making sure that the shapeshifter wasn't there.

He figured that he better stop by the witch doctor's hut to see what he was doing. He knew that he was going to have a long walk ahead of him.

To get to the witch doctor s hut but he decided to do it anyway. The roar from a lion motivated him, and he started running.

Sometime later he came upon the witch doctor's hut, he entered the witch doctor's hut and saw that he was hard at work.

You mustn't be here because there's a good chance that the shapeshifter will come after me here.

Go now and retreat into the hut next door, Sipho quickly retreated into the hut. The two headed lion walked away and the giant crocodile was following behind him. The lion knew that it was going to take a while to get the massive crocodile to the witch doctor's hut.

The witch doctor gathered up the elixirs and headed out to find the shapeshifter. An hour later he came to where the giant crocodile was and he was terrified to see the 2 headed lion which was looking at him.

He threw the 2 goat stomach pouches that were full of the elixir at the crocodile as it was coming after him with its mouth open.

Then there was a purple poof of smoke, and the shapeshifter was gone. The 2 headed lion saw that the witch doctor was safe and ran off, not to be seen again.

The next day the village people came out of hiding and returned to their village. He was celebrated by the village, and for dinner they had a large feast of fish. The witch doctor was made a defender, of the tribe.

Zulu Warriors

Zulu Shield

Zulu Hut

Zulu miners posing in Diamond Mine

Zulu Hunter

www.ingramcontent.com/pod-product-compliance
Lightning Source LLC
Chambersburg PA
CBHW040948110726
48006CB00007B/1305